Please Stay Here

I Want You Near...

Written by Dr Sarah Mundy

Illustrations by Rachel Millson-Hill

Information For Parents

Your little ones may bring you lots of fun and laughter, but there are often tricky times during the early years. As parents we can struggle with everyday challenges, especially when our children are aged between two and four. Whilst there is plenty of advice out there, the child's voice is often missed within this.

As a Consultant Clinical Psychologist, I have worked with many children and families over the last 20 years, supporting them with their emotional and behavioural wellbeing. What has become increasingly clear to me is the importance for young children to have their experiences understood, and to have parental help in making sense of them. Despite this, it can be hard to know how to talk to our children about what is going on for them, particularly when we are trying to manage big feelings and behaviours that they (and we) find difficult.

When I became a mum, I (naively) assumed that, given my clinical experience, I would know what to do when my son reached toddlerhood. The reality took me by surprise! I searched for innovative ways to provide a platform for young children to reflect upon, and learn from, their experiences. I was particularly interested in work that translated psychological models of child development into practice, with a focus upon those I frequently used in my work, namely attachment theory and storytelling.

I struggled to find stories to read with my son which were designed to enhance our relationship, and to help him (and me) make sense of his often confusing and overwhelming experiences. I therefore thought I would try to write some myself - hence this series!

Bartley's Books are a series of interactive picture books for young children and their parents, written to support families through some of those common, but tricky, situations we all experience in early childhood. There are six stories within the first series, focusing upon separation anxiety, tricky behaviour, bedtime routines, healthy eating, toilet training and the arrival of a new sibling.

As well as the illustrated story, each book includes "Top Tips" for managing the specific situation. If you are interested in the theory behind this series - and would like additional ideas to put into practice - a *Parenting Handbook* is available separately. The handbook considers how best to support your child's emotional and behavioural development throughout their early years (and beyond).

The stories feature Bartley Bear (and his parents) learning to cope with, and understand, his world. There's also a curious squirrel called Nudge around to help (you just have to find him under the flaps!). There are lots of opportunities within the book where you can talk about your own child's experiences and there are a number of prompter questions (asked by Nudge) to help you do this.

How To Read The Stories With Your Child

You can be creative and flexible with the stories; they have been developed to promote discussion, both about Bartley's experiences and also your child's, rather than to follow a rigid script. Feel free to leave out the prompter questions completely, answer them yourself, or add more…it's up to you. Just try to follow your child's lead and go at their pace.

Although the books focus upon tricky situations, try to keep the atmosphere light-hearted and playful – children learn best when they feel at ease and through stories that are engaging and fun. It is also helpful if you convey the emotional content of the story non-verbally as well as verbally.

I am aware that not all children have a mum and/or a dad – it's fine to adapt Nudge's questions to fit with your own family make-up.

Separation Anxiety

Separation anxiety is a common experience for little ones. *Please Stay Here - I Want You Near* is written to help children understand and cope with spending time away from their parents, whether it be with childminder or nanny, at nursery, pre-school or 'big' school. It may be helpful if those looking after your child also read this book with them. This will encourage a common approach and help your child to learn that other adults, in different settings, are also interested in their experiences.

This is
Bartley Bear

He isn't very old –
Mostly he is happy,
sometimes he is bold.

As he climbed into his rocket
Mum said, "Let's be on our way."
"But, Mum," he said, "it's out of fuel:

"There's no take off today!"

9

Even though he liked school,
Leaving Mum was tough.

His tummy felt funny and tied in knots,
he just didn't feel brave enough.

11

Mum knew that he was worried
and gave him a big bear hug.
She said he could bring a toy with him:
He chose his astronaut – Doug.

It was nearly time to take off,
their journey had begun:
Shoes on, off they went...

5.4.3.2.1!

With Mum and Doug on board,
Bartley steered around the bends.

They **Zoomed**

past a planet and overtook
some friends.

14

But when they got to school
Bartley wasn't sure.
He stopped, looked up at Mum,
and hid behind the door.

"Let's go and see what's out," said Mum.
"Now, what is there to play?
Doug can have a look around.
I'm back later today."

Mum gave his little paw a squeeze,
he lent in for a cuddle.
"Hey, there's lovely Mrs Cook,
blowing great **big, bouncy**
bubbles!"

17

Bartley held his mum real close
as Mrs Cook came over.
"Hi there, we're building rockets.
Can you help me make a Rover?"

Bartley looked around
and, by him on the floor,
a pile of **sparkly, shiny** bits –
gizmos and **gadgets galore!**

And then he spotted Sandy –
his favourite little friend.
She smiled and said, "Come on Bart,
help me build this end!"

20

They were sticking on a handle
When Mum said goodbye.
He wanted her to be with him:
"please stay
and watch this fly."

"I can't my love, I have to work –
I know it's hard for you."
Bartley waved, "OK. Bye, Mum."
He didn't know what to do.

22

Mrs Cook came over
to help him settle in.
She bent down, held his paw
and stroked his furry chin.

23

"Your rocket looks spectacular.
Should Doug steer the craft?"
She put him in the driver's seat:
This made Bartley laugh.

Bartley then played outside
on the bikes with Ben;
they went around the playground
again and again and again.

25

Next they read a story,
about a silly bunny.
Can you guess what happened?
It was very, very **funny!**

I CAN TELL
THE TIME!

School was nearly over...
The children ate their snacks
and before he'd even missed her
Bartley's Mum came back.

Bartley ran to meet her
with the rocket in his hand.
"I can't believe you made that –
Let's take it home to land."

When they got back home
he put his spaceman slippers on.
He told his mum about his day:
He was glad that he had gone.

Doug loved his brand new rocket,
he slept in it all night.
Bartley had an amazing dream
about their galactic flight.

Next time he would remember
that school was really fun,
and he would be just fine there
without his dad or mum.

Top Tips for Separation Anxiety

Talk to your child about what will happen at their childcare setting and let them know you will be back at the end (try to be on time to pick them up). Try to ensure you have a regular routine before and after childcare.

Try to transfer your child directly to a trusted adult in whatever setting their childcare takes place when you leave, so they have someone they trust to help them manage their feelings of anxiety and so they see you working together.

However tempting it is, don't sneak out or lie that you are just going to the loo! Remember that trust is key to your relationship with your child. A bit of distraction, with a clear message that you are going, is fine though.

Your child may have a favourite object or toy, which helps them to remember you and feel more at ease. Taking this with them can reduce anxiety around separation.

Take their feelings seriously – tell them that it is normal to feel worried (and sometimes angry), but that they will have fun when they are there.